This book belongs to:

....

This Orchard book belongs to

_____

_____

_____

For James Pomerance — MM

For Tom and Elliot — AA

ORCHARD BOOKS
Carmelite House
50 Victoria Embankment
London EC4Y 0DZ

First published in 2009 by Orchard Books
This edition First published in 2017
ISBN 978 1 40835 373 8

Text © Margaret Mayo 2009
Illustrations © Alex Ayliffe 2009

The rights of Margaret Mayo to be identified as the author
and Alex Ayliffe to be identified as illustrator of this work
have been asserted by them in accordance with the
Copyright, Designs and Patents Act, 1988.

A CIP catalogue record for this book
is available from the British Library.

1 3 5 7 9 10 8 6 4 2

Printed in China

Orchard Books is an imprint of Hachette Children's Group
Part of The Watts Publishing Group
an Hachette UK company.
www.hachette.co.uk

Sharks are good at snap, snap, snapping,

Whoosh! – dashing, tails lashing,

Spiky teeth ready for snap, snapping.

So snap, sharks, snap!

Dolphins are good at dance, dance, dancing,
High jumping, fast spinning,

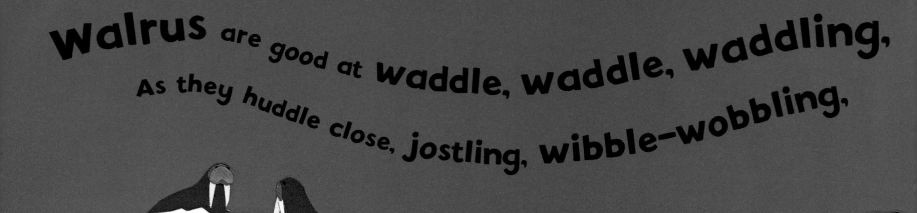

Walrus are good at **waddle, waddle, waddling,**
As they huddle close, jostling, wibble–wobbling,

Making such a noise – blah! blah! – bellowing!
So waddle, walrus, waddle!

Whales are good at **glide, glide, gliding,**
Tails going **up down, up down beating.**

As they blast out air – **pouffe!** – tall spouts **creating.**

So **glide**, whales, **glide!**

Sea otters are good at **float, float, floating.**
Lying on their backs, shellfish scrunch, scrunching,

Little pups cradling and quietly snoozing.

So float, sea otters, float!

Penguins are good at dive, dive, diving, swooping, swerving, quick zig-zagging,

Tails and feet guiding, stiff wings **flip-flapping.**

So **dive**, penguins, **dive!**

Polar bears are good at **lollop, lollop, lolloping,**

With cubs **following** . . .

Slipping, sliding and roly-polying!
So lollop, polar bears, lollop!

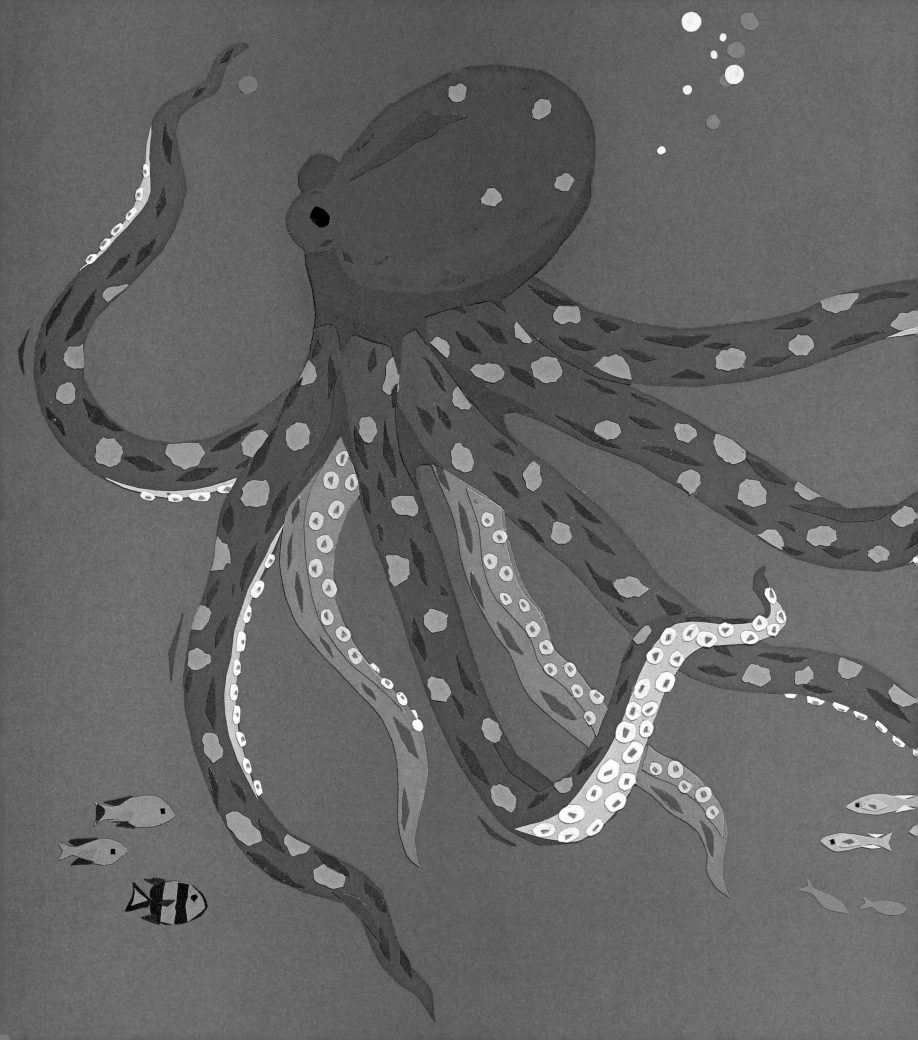

Octopuses are good at **waggle, waggle, waggling,**
Arms waving, food grabbing, **munch, munching,**
And – squish! – jetting off, long arms **trailing.**
So **waggle,** octopuses, **waggle!**

Stingrays are good at underwater **flying**,
Wide fins **sweeping**, ripple, **rippling**,

Spindly tails flicking and . . . stinging!
So fly, stingrays, fly!

Seals are good at **play, play, playing,** chasing, dodging and . . . ooohh! . . . somersaulting,

Coming to the surface and snorting.

So play, seals, play!

Sea turtles are good at dig, dig, digging,
Sand scoop scooping, safe nests making,

Eggs laying . . . more digging! . . . covering and hiding.
So dig, sea turtles, dig!

All these creatures are good at swimming,
But they can never live on the shore.

A snapping shark is one such creature.
Now look carefully – can you find some more?

To my boys, Hugo and Sam xx ~ RV

For Princess Natalie x ~ EE

Bloomsbury Publishing, London, New Delhi, New York and Sydney

First published in Great Britain in 2014 by Bloomsbury Publishing Plc
50 Bedford Square, London, WC1B 3DP

Text copyright © Rachel Valentine 2014
Illustrations copyright © Ed Eaves 2014

The moral rights of the author and illustrator have been asserted

A CIP catalogue record for this book is available from the British Library

ISBN 978 1 4088 3677 4 (HB)
ISBN 978 1 4088 3678 1 (PB)
ISBN 978 1 4088 3896 9 (eBook)

Printed in China by C&C Offset Printing Co Ltd, Shenzhen, Guangdong

1 3 5 7 9 10 8 6 4 2

www.bloomsbury.com

Marmaduke
the Very Different
Dragon

Rachel Valentine
Ed Eaves

BLOOMSBURY

LONDON NEW DELHI NEW YORK SYDNEY

Marmaduke was different.

The other dragons were purple with smooth shiny scales.
But Marmaduke was faded orange with sticky-out scales.

The other dragons had tiny neat ears.
But Marmaduke's ears . . . well they were enormous!

And while the other dragons loved to fly, Marmaduke didn't.
His wings were different. They were unusual.
And, because he didn't want anyone to see them, he never flew.

Marmaduke had always wanted to protect a princess,
but he'd never had the chance.

One day he asked the other dragons for help.

"You?" they laughed. "Protect a princess? Marmaduke, you don't even fly! Princesses need dragons like us, not you!"

Marmaduke wandered sadly through the woods when, suddenly, he spotted a tower with a beautiful princess leaning out of the highest window – and no dragon protecting her!

This is my chance! thought Marmaduke. Trembling, he called, "Excuse me! I don't suppose . . . I was wondering . . . Could I . . . be your dragon?"

The princess looked down. "You're not really a proper dragon, are you?" she sniffed. "You're not even the right colour. My daddy's getting a real dragon to keep me safe."

Poor Marmaduke.
He turned and ran, as fast as he could –
all the way to his cave, where he curled up on his bed.

"I don't like being different!" he sighed, as a tear rolled down his cheek.

But, a long way away, someone else was being different too – Princess Meg!

The other princesses were quiet with pretty dresses and neat hair. But Meg was loud with a crazy dress and very messy hair.

And while the other princesses sat calmly on their chairs, Meg **loved** to dance . . . in a most un-princess-like way!

None of the dragons wanted to protect Meg.
But she didn't mind.
"Who'd want to steal me?" she chuckled.
"I don't need a dragon!"

And Meg was happy – especially today.
Today she felt like dancing!

She discoed across the drawbridge,

leapt over logs,

twisted through tall trees
and danced away till dusk.

But Meg was having too much fun
and, as she boogied through the bushes,
she realised she was lost –
deep in the woods,
in the dark,
all alone.

"HELP!" she cried. "PLEASE HELP!"
But she was so far away that no one could hear her.

Or could they?
Because, a long way away, there **was** someone.
Someone with enormous ears,
someone who heard her . . .

Marmaduke!

He leapt out of his cave and galloped through the trees,
dashed across the rocks and hurtled round the bushes.

"I've come to rescue you!" Marmaduke puffed, proudly.

"Oh, thank you!" cried Meg.

Meg leapt on Marmaduke's back, ready to fly.
But Marmaduke started to run!
"I think flying would be quicker," said Meg.

"I . . . I don't fly," said Marmaduke, quietly.
"My wings don't look like other dragon wings, they're different."
"I'm sure they're fine," said Meg, kindly. "Why don't you show me?"

And so, very slowly, Marmaduke opened his wings.

Up, up they went, reaching to the sky –
the most **amazing** wings Meg had ever seen.

"Those **are** different!" gasped Meg,
as they shimmered and sparkled.
"Fantastically different! Beautiful!"

Marmaduke smiled, "Really?"
"Really!" shouted Meg. "Let's go!"

And up they soared.

As they reached Meg's tower, Marmaduke took a deep breath.
"I don't suppose you need a dragon to protect you?"
he asked, nervously.

Meg shook her head.
"Not really. You see, I'm not like other princesses!"

Marmaduke's face fell and he turned away sadly.

But then Meg smiled.
"I would like a friend though," she said.
"A wonderfully different friend!
A friend just like you!"

Marmaduke and Meg **were** different.
Fantastically, brilliantly, happily different . . . together.
The other dragons watched them, shaking their heads.

"Really, they're having too much fun," they grumbled.
"They're far too happy."

"I wish . . ." they each muttered,
"I wish . . . that I could be that different!"